OLD BEECH TREE

OLD BADGER SET

FARM ROAD

THE HOLLOW OAK

FOX DEN

MOLE HILLS

WILLOW POOL

THE MEADOW

OLD BRIDGE

THE RIVER

The author would like to thank Dr Gerald Legg
of the Booth Museum of Natural History, Brighton,
for his help and advice.

Text copyright © 1996 by Tessa Potter. Illustrations copyright © 1996 by Ken Lilly.
The rights of Tessa Potter and Ken Lilly to be identified as the author and illustrator of this work have been
asserted by them in accordance with the Copyright, Designs and Patents Act, 1988.
First published in Great Britain in 1996 by Andersen Press Ltd., 20 Vauxhall Bridge Road, London SW1V
2SA. Published in Australia by Random House Australia Pty., 20 Alfred Street, Milsons Point, Sydney, NSW
2061. All rights reserved. Colour separated in Switzerland by Photolitho AG, Offsetreproduktionen, Gossau,
Zürich. Printed and bound in Italy by Grafiche AZ, Verona.

10   9   8   7   6   5   4   3   2   1

British Library Cataloguing in Publication Data available.
ISBN 0 86264 442 9

This book has been printed on acid-free paper

Digger

THE STORY OF A MOLE

Story by Tessa Potter
Illustrations by Ken Lilly

Andersen Press • London

The first weeks of autumn were warm and golden.
Birds feasted on the hedgerows while small
animals searched for food, preparing for the cold
months ahead. The rabbits on Burrow Down
enjoyed the last warmth of the sun.

But now the skies were dark and a cold wind swept across the Down, bringing rain and hail. The birds and animals took shelter where they could. A young fox took refuge among the roots of an old tree.

A young heron sat hunched on the river bank, staring hopelessly into the swirling, muddy water. It had been raining for seven days now and fishing was hard in the swollen river.

At last, a patch of light appeared
in the sky and the rain eased.
A wagtail landed on one of the small
piles of earth dotted over the meadow.
    A sudden movement sent the
little bird scurrying away. Fresh
earth was being thrown up —
Digger the mole was making a new
tunnel. The rain and cold had
not bothered Digger much. A little
water had seeped into her tunnel
but her nest was still warm and dry.

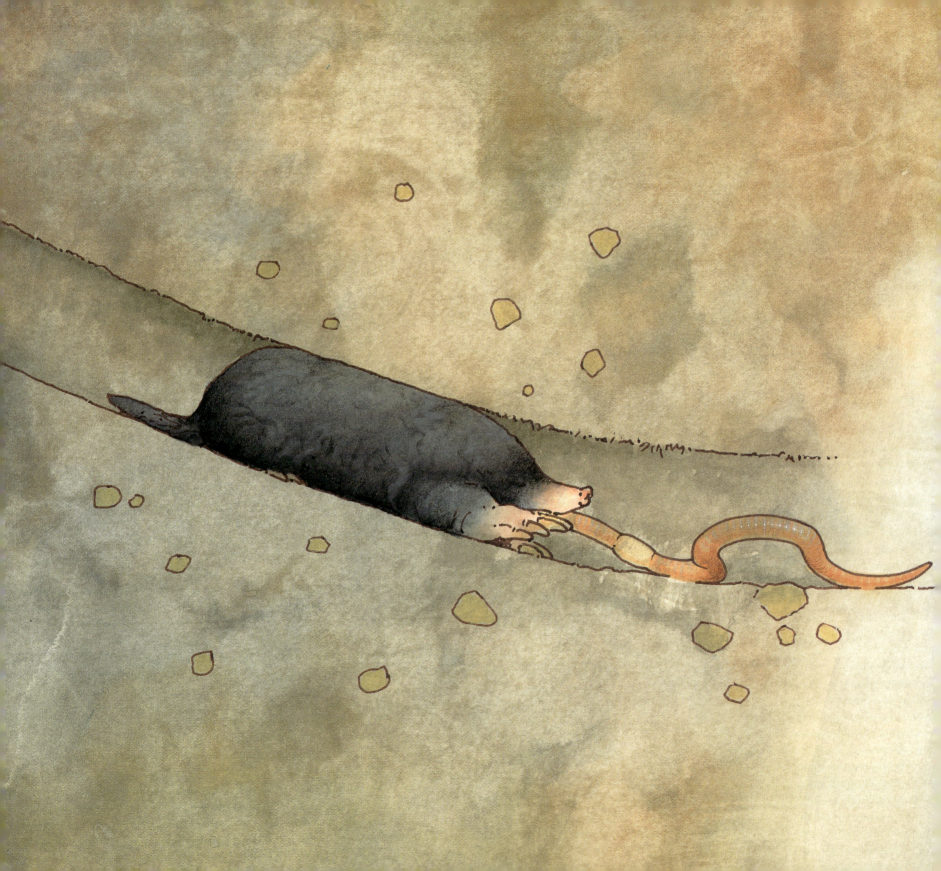

Digger was hungry after clearing so much earth, so she set off to look for food. She found an earthworm which had fallen through the tunnel wall. She snapped its head off and then sucked it up, guiding its long body between her front paws. Then she cleaned her fur, made herself comfortable in her nest and went to sleep.

Outside, the sky had grown dark again and huge drops of rain were falling. The heron gave up his fishing.

Then the storm broke. Lightning flashed across the sky. The wind raged and the rain poured down in torrents. Slowly, the swirling river crept higher and higher over the reeds and rushes, until at last it broke its banks. The water swept out across the Meadow.

In her underground nest,
Digger was woken by a
trickle of water. Then,
suddenly, water was
roaring through her
tunnels. She scrambled
out of her nest and swam
towards a shaft which led
up to the Meadow. She
had to get out. She
clawed upwards, trying
to reach the surface, but
as she pulled the earth
away, more water rushed
through the hole,
washing her back down.
She was under water
now. She couldn't
breathe.

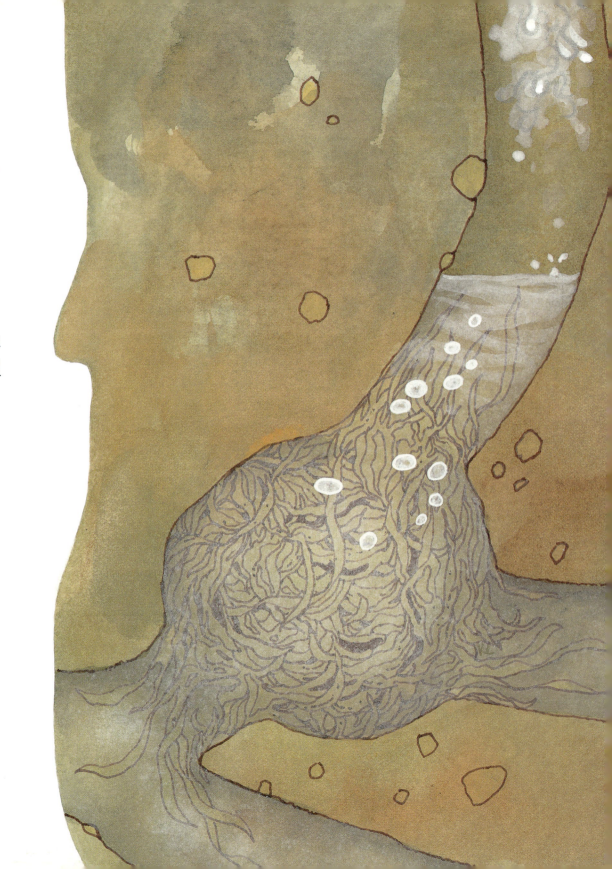

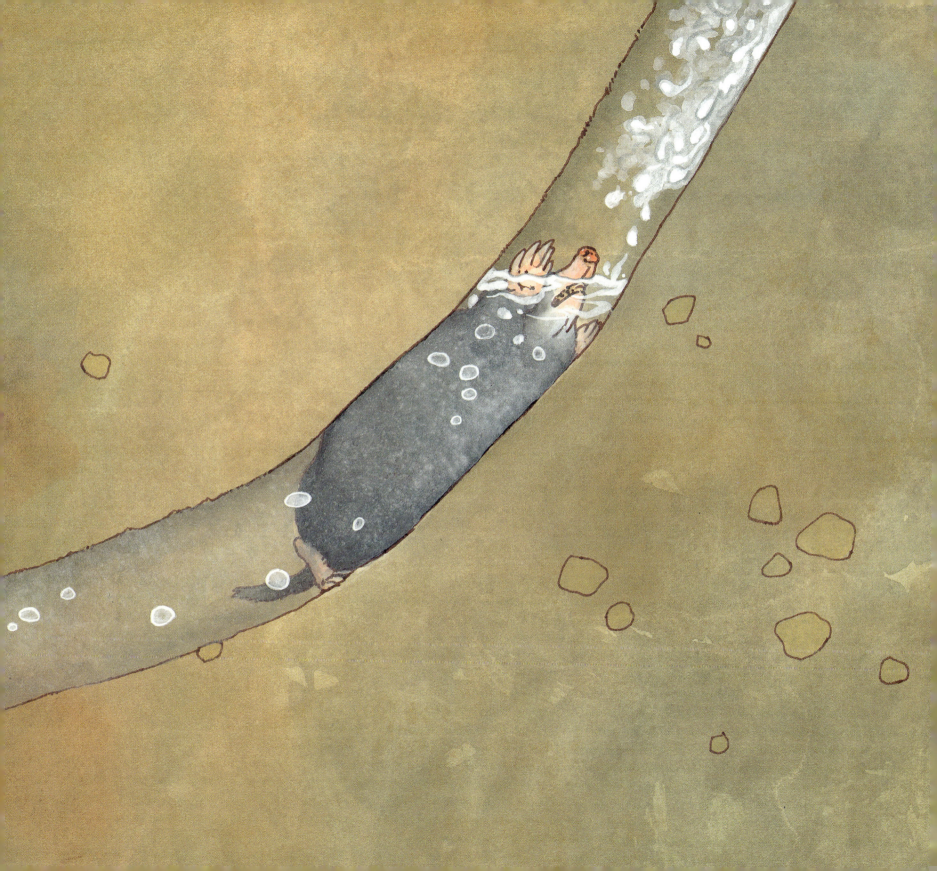

Desperately, Digger swam with
her powerful front legs until
at last she managed to pull herself
up through the hole. She gulped
the cold air, paddling hard to keep
afloat. The whole of the Meadow
was under water. All around, other
small creatures were trying
to reach dry land.

Digger headed with all her strength towards the high ground. She knew that as the wind dropped, the hunters would appear, looking for easy prey. For a second a dark shape hovered right above her. Digger was terrified. But the bird wheeled away as something else caught his eye.

Finally, shivering and exhausted,
Digger dragged herself onto the land.
The heron was wading in the
shallows. He'd just caught a water shrew
so he didn't notice Digger as
she slipped by and disappeared
into the Great Wood.

It was night when Digger woke. Everything was still and the flood water lay like a dark mirror over the Meadow. Nearby, a young otter explored the shallow water.

Digger needed food and proper shelter urgently. She couldn't go back to her tunnels under the Meadow. So that night Digger set out through the Great Wood to find a new home.

Look back at the story.
Can you find…

A **bank vole** eating a rosehip.

A **blackbird** eating a blackberry.

A **split hazelnut** on the squirrel's feeding table.

A **wood mouse** carrying a hazelnut.

A **rabbit**.

A **shaggy inkcap**.

A **kestrel** hovering.

A **leatherjacket**. These underground larvae turn into craneflies.

A **four spotted orb web spider** in the middle of her web. If she catches an insect, she bites it with her fangs then ties it up in silk.

A **fly agaric**. These fungi are very poisonous.

A **sycamore seed** spinning to the ground.

A **common toad** hiding. The toad will hibernate all winter.

A **grey heron** catching a water shrew.

A **wolf spider** hunting a harvestman. The harvestman has escaped, leaving the spider holding his wriggling leg.

A **honey fungus**. What animal is eating this fungus?

A **grey squirrel** eating a puffball.

A **jay** burying some acorns. Some of the nuts will be forgotten and will grow into new trees in spring.

A **boletus** (Cep). In the autumn fungi provide food for many animals.

An **otter**.

An **earthworm** in the mole's worm store. The mole bites off the worm's head to stop it burrowing away.

A **hammock spider's web**. A cranefly has bumped into the spider's threads and fallen into the hammock.

A **blackthorn berry**.

A **water shrew** being caught by a heron.

A **rosehip**.

THINGS TO DO

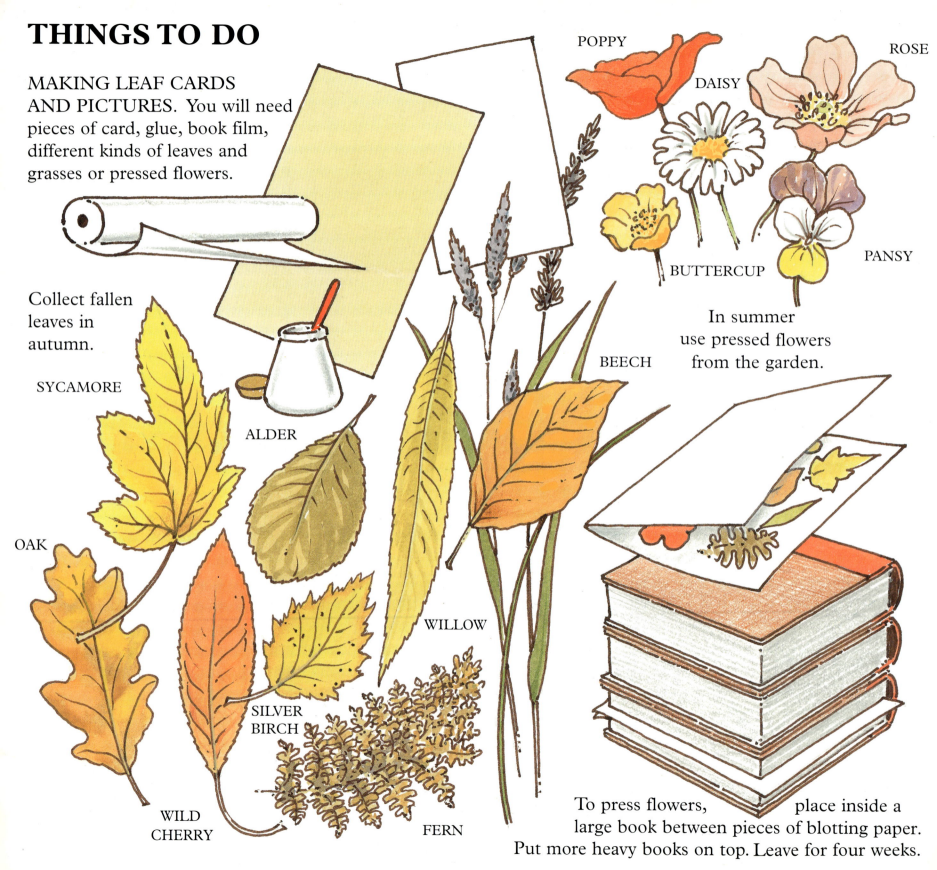

MAKING LEAF CARDS AND PICTURES. You will need pieces of card, glue, book film, different kinds of leaves and grasses or pressed flowers.

Collect fallen leaves in autumn.

SYCAMORE

ALDER

OAK

WILD CHERRY

SILVER BIRCH

FERN

WILLOW

BEECH

POPPY

DAISY

ROSE

BUTTERCUP

PANSY

In summer use pressed flowers from the garden.

To press flowers, place inside a large book between pieces of blotting paper. Put more heavy books on top. Leave for four weeks.

BIRTHDAY
CARD

PICTURE

BOOK MARK

Stick the leaves,
grasses or flowers
carefully onto the
card and cover
with book film.

CHRISTMAS CARD

CALENDAR